Through the Seasons With Macy

Written and Illustrated by :
Christine Kuschewski

This book is dedicated to my great niece and nephews. I love you with all my heart!

There are four seasons in a year. The first is spring, followed by summer, fall and winter.

In spring, new life begins.
Flowers bloom and the
leaves on the trees bud.

Baby animals are also born in the spring. Can you see the ducklings?

Can you see the bunnies?

The weather begins to get warm in the spring. Macy loves to wear her pretty dress.

We celebrate Easter in the spring. Macy found so many eggs!

In summer, the trees and grass are green.

We celebrate the 4th of July during the summer. Fireworks, parades and flags!

The weather in summer is hot. Macy wears her swim suit.

Macy likes to swim in the pool. The water helps keep her cool.

In fall, the leaves turn colors, and pumpkins are picked.

The weather turns cooler,
and Macy needs to wear
her flannel.

We celebrate Halloween and Thanksgiving in the fall.

We watch football in the fall, too. Macy's favorite team is the Green Bay Packers!

Winter is the last season of the year. It is cold in winter. Macy wears her winter coat.

Many places get snow in the winter. You can go sledding, skiing or ice skating. You can also make snowballs like Macy did.

We celebrate Christmas and the new year in winter.

Can you name each season?
Look at Macy to see what she
is wearing.

Christine Kuschewski has been a special education teacher for 22 years. She loves teaching children how to read. Her love for books and education has led her to writing children's books.

Christine and Macy live in Arizona. Macy loves to spend time with her best friends, Toby, Kona and their family. Macy is a 7 year-old Bichon Frise, Poodle, Maltese and Shih-Tzu mix. Everyone who meets Macy falls in love with her. Together Christine and Macy enjoy spreading love to the world.

Love Queen
LET YOUR LOVE SHINE THROUGH

Macy's World Titles

Made in the USA
Columbia, SC
22 November 2022

71015348R00024